FRACTURED

FRACTURED

J. A. Springs

This is a work of fiction. Names, characters, places, and incidents are the product of the author's imagination or are used fictitiously. Any resemblance to actual persons, living or dead, or actual events is purely coincidental.

Dedication

Life will sometimes fracture us in to bits but it's up to us to put the pieces together. When we do, we can be stronger.

I dedicate this work to my brother for giving me the idea for this narrative.

1

The cityscape shimmered in a dazzling display of neon hues, a breathtaking symphony of lights that painted the blended real and virtual world in a vivid tapestry. Implants within the citizens, seamlessly connecting them to this alternate reality. Hovering drones streaked across the sky, leaving trails of luminescent streaks that crisscrossed above the bustling streets. The air was alive with the hum of technology and the chatter of people engaging in real and virtual conversations.

Amidst this kaleidoscope of colors and sounds, Alex navigated the crowded streets. His implants, like those of everyone around him, were the conduits to this mesmerizing world. They allowed information to flow seamlessly between reality and the virtual, creating a symbiotic relationship that defined everyday life. Alex's eyes, enhanced by the implants, perceived the world with an augmented vibrancy that transcended the mundane.

As Alex leisurely strolled through the bustling city, he relished the lack of a predetermined destination, allowing himself the freedom to wander through its vibrant streets. His surroundings teemed with a diverse array of individuals, each capturing a fragment of his attention. Notably, a middle-aged man guided his canine companion toward the nearby park, just beyond Alex's current location. A short distance away, the cries of a newborn echoed, prompting a young woman to pause. With a gentle touch, she lifted the infant from the stroller, soothing whatever ailed him or her in her comforting embrace. The dynamic city scenes unfolded around Alex, offering glimpses into the lives and interactions of its diverse inhabitants.

With a smile, Alex embraced the unfolding tapestry of life around him, finding pure joy in the simple act of existence. Every day held the promise of something new to experience, even within the seemingly mundane tasks that peppered his routine.

As he stood on the street corner, patiently awaiting the change of the signal light that would grant him and others passage across the street, Alex's inadvertent encounter with a nearby pole disrupted his tranquility. In a moment of distraction, he bumped into the pole situated less than a foot away. Reacting swiftly, he withdrew his hand, startled by a faint shock, akin to a low current of electricity, coursing through his body. The unexpected jolt punctuated the otherwise routine moment, adding a subtle undercurrent of surprise to Alex's day.

Alex, inclined to dismiss the incident, found himself abruptly interrupted by a sudden glitch that disrupted his connection to the augmented realm.

"Ouch," Alex exclaimed as a sudden throb pulsed through his head. He closed his eyes tightly, leaning forward to rub his temples with the palm of his hand in an attempt to alleviate the pain. Although he knew such remedies seldom worked, it was a reflexive act driven by human nature. Despite providing little relief, the pain gradually subsided, and Alex opened his eyes again.

Surveying the world around him, Alex was met with disbelief, even a hint of shock. In just a few moments, everything seemed to have changed. Fearing that his eyes might be deceiving him due to the lingering headache, he clasped them shut once more, rubbing them before cautiously reopening them to reassess the altered reality.

"This can't be right," Alex said slowly and cautiously, a reluctance evident in his words as he grappled with the disbelief of what lay before him. Attempting to deny the stark reality unfolding, he questioned, "What happened?" After another few moments passed, and his surroundings persisted unchanged from moments before he rubbed his eyes, he voiced his inquiry once more.

Colors dulled, and the once-vibrant surroundings turned into a monochrome landscape. Panic flickered in Alex's eyes as he attempted to access the augmented interface, but the world around him stubbornly resisted. It was as if a curtain had fallen, separating him from the vibrant tapestry that had woven itself into the fabric of his existence.

Frustration and confusion etched across Alex's face as he tried to make sense of this sudden disconnect. The once-familiar city had lost its luster, reduced to a dull palette of grays and browns. Buildings, once alive with holographic displays, now stood as monolithic structures devoid of personality. Even the people around him appeared as mere silhouettes, their vibrant avatars erased.

Disoriented, Alex slipped and tumbled to the ground, questioning the accuracy of his senses. As he sat crumpled on the pavement, a fleeting doubt crossed his mind, suggesting he might be mistaken about what he was witnessing. However, the thought quickly gave way to frustration as he cursed the apparent failure of his implant.

A helping hand extended towards Alex, reaching down to assist him. "You alright, buddy?" inquired a handsome young man, his posture partially bent as he offered aid to lift Alex to his feet.

Blankly, Alex looked up, his thoughts still muddled. He shook his head slowly, attempting to clear the mental fog. "Yeah," he mumbled. "Just a little dizzy."

Alex accepted the offered hand, using it to pull himself back onto his feet. He brushed off his pants and turned to express his gratitude to the young man who had helped him. To his surprise, he found that the young man had already ventured off to rejoin the group he evidently belonged to. As they walked away, Alex caught snippets of their conversation.

"Why did you stop just a second ago?" queried one friend.

"I was... helping someone?..." the young man began, his voice trailing off in confusion that evolved into a question. It seemed as if he contemplated turning back the way he had come from to verify what he thought had happened, but midway through the turn, he stopped.

"Nothing. Let's go," he stated, falling into step behind the rest of his friends.

After they moved away, Alex ceased paying attention to their conversation. His focus had waned, especially after confirming that the young man had departed without the chance for Alex to express his gratitude. Deciding it was time to head home, somewhere he could safely assess his condition, he turned and surveyed each direction. It dawned on him that he wasn't sure which way led to his home.

Anxiety gripped Alex as he spun around, scanning each of the cardinal directions in search of a clue that might jog his memory. In his current predicament, he attempted to discern the general direction from which he had come, hoping that retracing his steps could revive his faltering memory. Yet, this effort, too, proved futile as he struggled to recall anything beyond the act of crossing the street.

In this disorienting state, Alex grappled with an unsettling realization—his memory was slipping away. Faces blurred, and the details of his own life became elusive fragments. He reached out to touch the holographic interface that had become an extension of his consciousness, only to find emptiness. The symbiosis that once defined him was now a fractured connection, leaving him adrift in a world stripped of its digital embellishments.

"What the hell is going on?" Alex muttered under his breath, uncertainty evident in his tone. "What do I do now?"

As Alex stood in the midst of the colorless city, the weight of his sudden isolation pressed upon him. The vibrant augmented world, once a comforting companion, now eluded his grasp. The challenge of reconstructing his identity in this stark reality unfolded before him, an unexpected journey into the depths of memory and the unknown.

2

The outside world now greeted Alex with an unwelcome palette of grays and browns. The city, once alive with vibrant hues, had succumbed to a monochrome malaise. Buildings stood like stoic sentinels, their exteriors drained of color, and the streets below echoed with the muted footsteps of pedestrians. Even the sky, usually a canvas of possibilities, seemed trapped in an eternal, featureless overcast.

Without his augmented reality interface, Alex stood rooted in place. It wasn't only the absence of his interface that halted him; a lack of awareness regarding where to go was equally paralyzing him. With no recollection of a destination or a retreat route, he found himself stuck, akin to a sailboat adrift without the wind to propel it forward.

In an effort to regain composure, Alex took deep breaths. "There's no need to panic. I can work this out. It's just going to take a bit of time," he reassured himself, summoning courage and motivation through self-directed words.

Alex chose a direction at random and set off. "As long as I move my feet, I'll arrive at a destination," he reasoned. Uncertain of where he would ultimately end up, he was certain that standing still on the sidewalk like a lamp post was not a viable option.

As Alex walked through the desaturated cityscape, a sense of desolation clung to every feature. The automated cars, now indistinguishable from one another, rolled along the streets like mechanical ghosts. The absence of signs robbed the storefronts of their individuality, transforming once-distinct establishments into a homogenous blur. Shops, office spaces and cafes stood side by side, their facades stripped of personality, their existence reduced to mere functional entities. Navigating blindly through entry and exit points, with the uncertain hope of reaching your intended destination, was the challenge ahead. This implied taking a gamble, a prospect that had never appealed to Alex.

The augmented reality overlay facilitated by the neural implants had long since erased the need for physical markers and replaced them with intangible digital equivalents. No longer did vibrant signs beckon to passersby, guiding them to hidden gems or familiar landmarks. Instead, the city now seemed like a labyrinth of uniformity, a place where every corner blended seamlessly into the next, creating a disorienting sense of sameness. It was a dull, oppressive monotony on the city streets now, everywhere that his gaze fell.

The augmented reality overlay had rendered such concerns obsolete and outdated. Now, without access to virtual reality, distinguishing one storefront from another proved overwhelmingly challenging. Alex chose not to vocalize the unflattering thoughts swirling in his mind regarding the absence of storefront identification. He understood that airing his grievances wouldn't alter his current predicament. Resorting to curses would serve no purpose other than indulging in a self-serving act, an acknowledgment that he needed to focus on navigating the challenging situation he found himself in.

Initially contemplating a stop for coffee as he sifted through his thoughts to recollect his identity, Alex realized the futility of that idea. Much like his identification, his finances were virtual, and he had no means to pay for any services. The loss of his interface left him not only destitute but also perpetuated his state of being lost, as he couldn't uncover his identity or address. The coexistence of these two states made the idea of finding a shop—now, one he couldn't even identify to save his life—utterly pointless for all practical purposes.

Alex's footsteps echoed against the concrete as he moved through the city's drab expanse. With his head lowered, Alex watched his footsteps as he moved forward. The absence of vibrant colors made the environment oppressive, casting a shadow over the once-bustling streets. Even the people he passed by appeared as walking silhouettes to him, their features obscured by a lack of visual diversity. Faces, once distinct and full of character, were now reduced to anonymous shapes in a grayscale world. Natural creations alone retained their vibrant colors, yet even these appeared equally subdued without the enhancement of the augmented overlay.

At one point, something caught Alex's attention, something he couldn't bring himself to accept as real. Up ahead on the sidewalk, an individual crossed the street. The person did so at the correct time and from the appropriate location, but that wasn't what drew Alex's focus. What stood out was that the individual appeared to be uniformly grey from head to toe, including their skin tone and hair color. Alex dismissed it as a product of his imagination, likely a result of the stress, and continued walking.

As he reached the next intersection, Alex couldn't help but feel a sense of longing for the dynamic city that once thrived with individuality. The stark reality surrounding him seemed like a barren canvas, devoid of the rich tapestry that had once defined the urban landscape. The augmented virtual display facilitated by the implant had overlaid itself onto reality but was now defunct, erasing the very essence that made each street corner unique.

In this colorless reality, Alex's world had become a canvas of monotony, a place where the absence of vibrancy mirrored the void left by his lost memories. The once-thriving city now stood as a testament to the consequences of a world where the virtually augmented and the real converged, blurring the lines between the tangible and the intangible, and leaving behind a cityscape drained of life and individuality.

3

The city park offered a temporary refuge from Alex's aimless wandering. He spotted a place along his path where he could rest. As he settled on his decision to occupy the weathered bench beneath the sprawling branches of an ancient oak, he pondered his next move. The notion of heading to a police station floated in his mind. Surely, they could help him unravel the mystery of his identity, but the more he contemplated, the less appealing the idea became.

His mind conjured a stereotype: only criminals lacked implants or knew how to disable them. Those without the world's ubiquitous neural interface were often relegated to the ghettos beyond the metropolitan sprawl, where crime thrived in tandem with poverty. The fear of being mistakenly labeled a criminal and banished to such a place gnawed at Alex's thoughts, casting a shadow over the police station plan.

"This is crazy. I'm not a criminal," Alex whispered. "But without a way to prove who I am, that doesn't really matter."

With a heavy sigh, he conceded to the reality of his situation, openly admitting, "I'm hungry." His stomach, responding in kind, emitted an audible growl, a reminder of his immediate needs. Alex settled onto the inviting bench, adopting a posture that mirrored both his weariness and contemplation. He sprawled comfortably, draping his arms over the backrest, and allowed his head to loll lazily backward, directing his gaze upward into the sky. The ambient sounds of nearby pedestrians eventually prompted him to sit up.

His attention was drawn by a passing couple, not because of the people themselves but by the hand-held food in the man's grasp, captivating his gaze like a moth to a flame. As he observed the ebb and flow of people passing by, his mind returned to the pressing issue of hunger. Another rumble from his stomach spurred him into acknowledging the limited options at his disposal. He sat with a futile hope, reaching into his pocket despite the knowledge that he carried no cash. The search yielded disappointment, and frustration crept into his expression.

Leaning forward with his head hung low, Alex's gaze fell upon something lying on the ground. A twenty-dollar bill lay there, as if fate had intervened in response to his plight. Slowly, he picked it up, glancing around to ensure no one was about to claim the money. A quick survey revealed no interested parties, providing him with a subtle sense of relief.

However, as he pocketed the unexpected windfall, his attention was diverted by a peculiar sight on the far side of the park. Another individual, entirely grey from head to toe, further along in the park and moving away from Alex's location. Discomfort settled within him, a subtle unease sparked by the anomaly. The person seemed like a glitch in the reality he once knew.

"What the hell is that?" Alex pondered. "That's the second person I've seen that looks like that."

Alex, attempting to rationalize the bizarre encounter, attributed it to his faulty implant playing tricks on him.

"Seeing people like that could be a result of the implant failing. That's gotta be it," Alex murmured.

Yet, the nagging doubt lingered. Standing up, he resolved to walk, the twenty-dollar bill now securely in his pocket. His destination remained uncertain, but he hoped to identify a place amid the dull and indistinct storefronts lining the city walk where he could satiate his hunger with a meal and coffee, the reassuringly familiar in a world that had turned strangely alien.

As Alex walked through the city, the idea of seeking medical assistance for his implant and memory issues took root in his mind. Surely, he reasoned, this type of failure must have occurred before to someone else. Recalling that contemporary doctors routinely performed maintenance on implants, he envisioned a solution to his predicament.

Musing over the prospect of a doctor's intervention, Alex considered the possibility of having his implant examined and repaired. If that course of action failed to yield results, he decided, a visit to the police station would be the next step. The thought of spending the entire day wandering the city, grappling with fragmented memories, and attempting to piece together his identity was unappealing. Alex was determined to find a more direct and efficient solution to his predicament.

The realization struck him: the primary obstacle to his plan was figuring out how to reach a doctor. Navigating the city's transformed landscape presented challenges, especially without the aid of his once-reliable implant. Determined to overcome this hurdle, Alex continued his journey, eyes scanning the surroundings for any indication of a medical facility that could potentially restore the missing fragments of his identity.

A resonant grumble echoed in Alex's ears as he clutched his spasming stomach. The audible protest from his belly prompted a reconsideration of the order of priorities for his missions. Deciding that a visit to the doctor's office could wait, he acknowledged that taking a few minutes to satiate his hunger wouldn't result in any significant lost time.

Alex's quest for sustenance led him to follow his nose, a sensory guide amidst the visual ambiguity. He found himself swept along by the ebb and flow of people, drifting into various establishments until he finally settled upon what seemed to be a suitable place.

Upon entering, however, a new set of challenges presented themselves. The counter stood unmanned, devoid of any human presence. Alex's initial confusion morphed into realization – his faulty implant was likely playing tricks on his perception. A virtual projection, an AI, was likely operating the cash register, rendering it invisible to his naked eyes.

Stranded without his implant, Alex faced another hurdle – the menu, normally displayed digitally, was now a blank slate to him. The only visible entities were the workers behind the counter, seamlessly orchestrating their tasks in harmony with automated processors. Undeterred, he approached the counter, calling out for assistance.

A reluctant figure emerged, eyes reflecting irritation at the interruption. Alex hesitated, crafting a cover story to shield the true nature of his predicament. The worker, though dubious, accepted the excuse, prompting Alex to inquire about his options with a twenty-dollar bill in hand.

The response was straightforward – a sandwich and a coffee. Alex nodded in agreement, attempting to pass the bill to the disgruntled worker. However, instead of acceptance, the man's expression twisted into disgust at the sight of the paper currency.

"Why are you using this?" he scoffed, eyeing the bill with disdain.

"I'm trying to pay for my meal," Alex said, a puzzled expression on his face.

"With this," the man said, his nose upturned in disgust. "I don't even wanna touch that thing. Where did you even get it from?"

Caught off guard, Alex stood there, feeling dumbfounded. The man's remark struck a chord – paper money was an outdated relic in a world that had moved on. As Alex grappled with the realization, the man's frustration bubbled over. He continued to question Alex's choice, expressing his disdain for the rare sight of paper currency in the modern world.

"I don't have any other way to pay for the meal," Alex admitted, a tinge of embarrassment coloring his cheeks.

With a mix of annoyance and anger, the worker declared their refusal to accept the archaic form of payment. There was no change available, and the man's tone grew more heated as he dismissively handed over the order, instructing Alex not to worry about payment. A baffled Alex stood there, caught off guard by the unexpected confrontation, watching as the disgruntled worker stomped away, leaving him to contemplate the bizarre encounter in the midst of the bland and indifferent surroundings of the city.

4

The crowded coffee shop buzzed with the hum of conversations, clinking cups, and the hiss of the espresso machine. Alex sat alone at a corner table, staring into the swirls of his untouched latte. He had become an unintentional observer in a world that seemed to move around him, blissfully unaware of his presence.

Alex glanced down at his partially consumed sandwich and the twenty-dollar bill resting beside it. He addressed the money with a wry tone, "I thought my luck had changed when I found you. I guess I was wrong. It's hard to find places to spend the likes of you nowadays."

As the absurdity of conversing with an inanimate object struck him, Alex felt the urge to laugh. Yet, he quickly suppressed the impulse, realizing that, given his current mental state, laughter might seamlessly transform into tears. With a swipe at his eyes to stave off the threatened tears, he acknowledged the precariousness of his emotional balance.

He collected his thoughts, then metaphorically gathered the remnants of his meal. Holding the remains in one hand, he glanced down at the twenty-dollar bill. A wave of disappointment and anger washed over him, and he considered leaving the almost useless currency where it lay. After a brief moment of reflection, he angrily scooped up the bill and stuffed it into his pocket.

As he stood to leave, the ambient chatter hushed momentarily. A few patrons turned their heads, their eyes catching an ephemeral glimpse of Alex. But as he made his way towards the exit, it was as if an invisible veil descended. Conversations resumed, and gazes shifted back to the steaming cups and glowing data interfaces scattered across the tables.

Out on the bustling sidewalk, Alex paced amidst the throng of faces, each absorbed in their individual worlds. A heavy groan escaped him, carrying the weight of a feeling of invisibility. It seemed as though he could traverse past acquaintances, colleagues, and friends, only to discover that his existence dissipated with each step away from their sight. An involuntary sigh slipped out, a soft acknowledgment of the cruel irony—he felt destined to be forgotten the moment he exited their field of vision.

Determined to proceed with his plans of seeking medical assistance for his malfunctioning implant, Alex recognized the need for information to guide him to a medical facility amid the monotonous surroundings.

In the nearby park he had previously visited, Alex noticed a group of friends engaged in lively conversation. Approaching cautiously, a flicker of hope ignited within him. As he drew nearer, their laughter softened, and for a fleeting moment, their eyes met his. However, upon stepping into their circle to inquire about directions, the laughter resumed, they turned away, and his presence seemed to dissolve into the background noise. It was a disconcerting experience—a delicate dance of inclusion and exclusion, leaving him on the fringes of connection that refused to solidify.

"Wow," Alex remarked sarcastically, misunderstanding their actions. He sensed intentional disregard. Scanning the surroundings, he muttered, "I'll find someone else to ask for directions."

Reluctantly, Alex conceded to himself that asking for directions was an outdated notion. It was an uncommon practice, especially with the convenience of neural implants. Even then, a data pad could provide the necessary internet-based information, but he found himself without one.

In a nearby boutique, Alex caught snippets of conversation between two women discussing an upcoming event. Anxious to seek guidance, he interjected casually, inquiring about the route to a nearby medical facility. The women exchanged puzzled glances, as if an unexpected gust of wind had disrupted their conversation. In the blink of an eye, their attention shifted, and Alex became a forgotten whisper in the air once more.

"This is getting absurd," Alex remarked, his frustration evident. In an unexpected move, he pinched his shirt, pulling it up near his nose. "Do I stink or something? It feels like everyone is avoiding me as if I'm contagious."

Undeterred, Alex made repeated attempts. Sometimes, he managed to introduce himself, relying on the sole piece of information retained in his memory—his name. However, it consistently ended with a sense of déjà vu, as if he had to repeat the process. Eventually, the outcome remained the same, with others seemingly forgetting he was even present, either walking away or completely ignoring him.

The struggle was not just in being unseen; it was in the persistent need to reintroduce himself, a Sisyphean task that wore on his spirit. Alex longed for a connection that didn't require a constant reminder of his existence. He yearned for the warmth of acknowledgment, the simple act of being remembered.

As the day unfolded, Alex moved through the city like a phantom. Faces blurred into a mosaic of indifference, their gazes sliding off him like water off glass. The weight of his forgotten existence settled on his shoulders, and with each passing encounter, the ache of isolation deepened. Yet, beneath the invisible shroud that cloaked him from the world, a flicker of resilience remained—a persistent whisper that urged him to forge connections, even in the face of constant oblivion. Communication was imperative for Alex. Without assistance from others, he couldn't navigate to his destination.

5

A mid the sea of indifferent faces, Alex's attempts to connect with people were met with consistent indifference. Frustration etched lines on his face as he grappled with the unsettling reality of being seemingly invisible to those around him.

Lost in his thoughts, Alex was startled when a soft voice broke through his isolation. A young woman stood before him, concern etched on her features. "Are you alright?" she asked, genuine worry in her eyes.

Alex's eyes lit up with surprise and joy, realizing someone had finally acknowledged his existence. At first, he was so overwhelmed by the unexpected encounter that he struggled to find words.

"I... I..." Alex stuttered, but he ultimately silenced himself with a deep, angry breath, forcing calm upon his agitated emotions.

The concern on the young woman's face deepened, and she asked again, "You look distressed. Are you okay?"

Collecting himself, Alex managed a grateful smile. "I'm just... a bit lost and confused," he admitted.

The young lady extended a cordial smile and introduced herself, saying, "I'm Joanne," as she reached out her hand for a greeting. "I can offer you my assistance if you need it. I was standing off over there," she continued, pointing to a space not far away, "and I could see your distress."

"It was that bad, huh?" Alex stated plainly, running his hand through his hair before letting it fall back beside him.

"Yeah," Joanne replied with a small giggle. "It's written all over your face. What do you need help with, if you don't mind me asking?"

As Alex poured out his story, Joanne listened empathetically. She understood the predicament caused by the loss of his neural implant and sympathized with his struggle. Determined to help, she offered to provide him with directions.

"If it's alright with you, I can help you get directions to where you need to go," she offered.

Alex's mood brightened. This was the assistance he had been seeking for the past hour. It felt like this angel had arrived at just the right time. The image of a halo sitting atop her head flashed in his mind, and he couldn't help but smile at the thought. With help now available, his mood had significantly improved.

"Thanks, I appreciate that," Alex said with ease.

Joanne paused for a moment, interfacing with her own neural implant to gather the information Alex needed. Her actions were seamless, a demonstration of the technology Alex had lost.

"Alright," she eventually began. "I've got it. The nearest medical facility isn't that far away. Will you be able to find it if I tell you the directions, or do you need me to go with you to make sure you don't get lost?"

Alex had to suppress the feeling of being coddled like a child who needed his hand held to get where he needed to go. He waved a hand dismissively and said, "Nah, I'll be fine with the directions." He also hoped that he'd be able to navigate in this world with no clear landmarks or signs indicating where he was. In reality, he was like a blind man trying to traverse unknown territory at the moment. The analogy didn't quite fit because he could actually see, but what he saw was the un-augmented world, with no guiding directions to distinguish one bland destination from another.

Joanne, ignorant of how Alex felt, gave him the directions. She even went so far as to ask him to repeat them back to her. While Alex was embarrassed to do so, he complied anyway, realizing that it was a necessity dictated by circumstances that couldn't be ignored.

With directions now relayed, Joanne turned to leave. The imagined halo Alex associated with her seemed to brighten with a subtle golden glow, surrounding her as his appreciation for her assistance grew. It contrasted starkly with the dull grey world he was now in.

"Thank you, Joanne. Thank you so much," Alex said. Gratitude filled Alex's voice as he thanked Joanne profusely. Watching her walk away, he couldn't shake the feeling that there was something different about her. Turning over her shoulder, Joanne waved goodbye. Alex continued to watch her and then shifted his gaze to the others that were walking past on the sidewalk. Something peculiar seemed to register just beyond his ability to comprehend. Joanne was halfway down the block when he finally realized what was off.

As Alex glanced at the other people on the street, he noticed a subtle shimmer surrounding their entire bodies, a golden glow. It wasn't so bright that it was immediately noticeable, but now that he did notice it, it was hard to ignore. Yet, when he looked back at Joanne, her shimmer appeared slightly blackened and less vibrant. It was almost nonexistent. He dismissed it as an optical illusion, a trick played by his malfunctioning implant. Determined to follow Joanne's directions, he walked off, grateful for the brief connection in a world that seemed to overlook him.

Alex walked with purpose, intent on reaching his destination and finding a solution to his implant problem. Recalling Joanne's kindness, he immediately associated her with his sister, and the thoughts triggered a throbbing pain in his head. It became so intense that he had to stop walking and squat down, fearing that his balance might fail, causing him to topple over.

Grasping his head with both hands, Alex whispered through gritted teeth, "I have a sister."

The pain intensified, gaining strength to the point where Alex felt like he might pass out. Wincing, he cinched his eyes tightly closed in an attempt to block out the sunlight, hoping it would alleviate some of the intense pain gathering behind his eyes.

In his half-blinded state, the world around Alex seemed to shift. He knew it wasn't a real shift but a change in perspective as he began to recall details. Memories rushed in, and he recalled being in a room.

The room was dimly lit, shadows playing on the walls as Alex sat alone, surrounded by faded photographs and forgotten mementos. He cradled his head in his hands, eyes closed, as if shutting out the conflicting memories that clamored for attention within his mind.

In the sepia-toned recollections, Alex saw his sister, a beacon of joy in his childhood. Her laughter echoed through the halls of their family home, her presence a constant source of comfort. Yet, as he delved deeper into the recesses of his mind, another version of the memory surfaced—a somber reality where his sister was conspicuously absent, leaving an un-fillable void. In these divergent memories, he grew up as an only child.

The emotional turbulence within Alex intensified as he grappled with the disparity between these two versions of his past. Were the moments of shared laughter and whispered secrets figments of imagination, or had they been erased from existence? The weight of uncertainty settled like an anchor in his chest, pulling him into a sea of conflicting emotions. Eventually his world went black.

6

Alex's consciousness slowly stirred, like a ship emerging from a thick fog. Blinking, he surveyed his surroundings, a dimly lit waiting room with sterile white walls that seemed unfamiliar. His disorientation heightened as he struggled to recall how he ended up here.

The murmur of indistinct voices buzzed in the background, creating an odd symphony that echoed in Alex's ears. He pivoted his head, scanning the room in search of something recognizable. A pang of anxiety tugged at him when the reality of his current predicament sank in—he had no idea how he arrived here.

As he fumbled with his thoughts, a distant sound tugged at his attention, growing louder with each passing moment. Someone was calling his name. "Alex! Alex!" The urgency in the repeated summons drew him back to the present.

He turned towards the source of the voice, and his gaze locked onto the approaching figure of a nurse. She emerged from behind the reception desk, her steps purposeful as she headed towards him. There was something oddly familiar about her but Alex was too confused to pay it much attention.

The nurse reached him and halted in front of where he was seated. "Are you Alex?" she inquired, her eyes fixed on his face.

Upon casting his gaze upward at her, the initial notion that swept through his mind was a resounding, "Wow, she's stunning." A momentary pause followed as he grappled with his own train of thought. "Just as attractive as that girl..." Alex hesitated, a subtle furrow creasing his brow. Unfortunately, the memory of the specific girl he had in mind slipped through his mental fingers, leaving him in a puzzling state of forgetfulness.

After a brief moment, Alex focused his attention on the nurse. Still grappling with the fog of confusion, he hesitated before answering the question that she had asked. "Yes, I'm Alex," he replied, his tone uncertain. "But I don't know how I got here. What is this place?"

"You walked in by yourself about ten minutes ago," the nurse informed him, a fleeting frown crossing her face, revealing her momentary concern for his confusion. She quickly dismissed it, attributing his disorientation to the aftermath of just waking up.

The nurse offered a reassuring smile, her eyes displaying a hint of empathy. "You're in the doctor's office. You woke up, and we've been trying to get your attention for a while. The doctor is ready to see you now."

"Oh," Alex responded. "Yeah, I guess I'm ready. Can you lead the way?"

"Sure," the nurse replied, choosing not to mention that she had been waiting on him for precisely that reason.

Turning, the nurse waited for Alex before guiding him toward the examination room where the doctor awaited.

Accepting the guidance, Alex stood and followed the nurse into the examination room. It was a brief stroll down the hallway, and the nurse refrained from glancing back to confirm that Alex was trailing behind. She assumed that once he stood, he would proceed as instructed. Opening the door, she stepped to the side, allowing Alex to enter, all the while offering him a friendly smile.

"Dr. Howard, your patient is here," the nurse called out into the room. The sound of a chair moving from behind a desk was followed by Alex being greeted by the man in question. The sudden awakening at the doctor's office felt surreal to Alex. Not comprehending how he got there was unsettling, but he hoped the doctor could help him overcome the issues he was facing. Alex reached out a hand in greeting to the approaching doctor.

"Hi, I'm Alex," he said.

Dr. Howard appeared so at ease in meeting Alex for the first time that it raised a question in Alex's mind—had they met before? The doctor's presence felt familiar, almost as if Alex had known him all his life. It was challenging for Alex to believe that this encounter marked their first meeting today rather than a continuation of a longstanding acquaintance.

"Dr. Howard," the doctor replied with a friendly smile. He shook Alex's hand, his grip firm and reassuring, guiding him further into the space. With a free hand, Dr. Howard pointed to a designated spot for Alex to sit in the exam room.

Alex settled onto the exam table, making an effort to find comfort on the slightly unforgiving surface.

The sterile environment seemed to accentuate the oddity of the situation. Apart from the examination table, a desk, and a chair, the room was relatively empty. Sunlight streamed through the windows, casting a bright glow across the space.

The mention of sunlight brought back a fleeting thought to Alex's mind. He turned to see the nurse exiting, a subtle glow enveloping her. It was as if a dim, shadowed version of the golden shimmer he had noticed on Joanne lingered here, creating an otherworldly ambiance.

As the nurse exited, leaving him alone in the room, Alex's gaze lingered on her fleeting silhouette. Her attractive features captured his attention, and he found himself contemplating the enigmatic glow that surrounded her. The puzzle of this subtle radiance continued to occupy his thoughts. When Alex turned his attention back to the doctor, he couldn't help but notice a similar glow around him—a faint radiance that mirrored what he had observed on those individuals who seemed unaffected by his unusual situation and were able to perceive him and not forget he existed in the next instant.

The door swung shut, revealing a man in a white coat, now all professional and ready to delve into the matter at hand. "Hello, Alex," he greeted once more. "I'm Dr. Benjamin Howard. Let's discuss what brought you here today."

In the sterile examination room, Alex took a deep breath before explaining to Dr. Howard the peculiar chain of events. "I experienced a slight electric shock, and then my implant just stopped working," he recounted. The doctor's eyebrows furrowed in a confused expression, and Alex interpreted it as surprise at the notion that a mild electric shock could lead to such a malfunction. After a thoughtful pause, Alex continued, "And now, I have memory issues. I can't recall much about myself, just my name. I think my vision might be affected too."

Dr. Howard hummed in understanding and moved toward his desk. From a drawer, he retrieved a small circular device and approached Alex. "Relax," the doctor instructed as he placed the device on Alex's head. "I'm going to scan the pathways in your mind." After a brief moment, Dr. Howard returned to his desk to review the results.

Returning to Alex, Dr. Howard remarked, "It's just as I suspected. There are anomalies that need to be corrected."

Concern flashed in Alex's eyes, prompting him to seek clarification, "Is it a serious issue? Will my memory be damaged permanently?"

Dr. Howard chuckled, dispelling Alex's worries, "No, no. It's not that serious. It can be cleared up within an hour or so. It's not that big of a deal."

Relieved, Alex responded, "Oh." Eager to resolve the problem, he inquired if they could proceed with the procedure immediately.

"Can we go ahead with the procedure right away?" he asked. "Do you need me to wait while you set up whatever equipment you need to fix it?"

Dr. Howard closed his eyes and shook his head. "Repair work like this needs a professional," he replied. However, the doctor delivered further news, saying, "Unfortunately, we don't handle specialized repairs like this here. You'll have to go to a designated repair facility."

Taking a moment to consider this, Alex also realized he couldn't pay for the services that had been rendered. "I can't pay right now. My implant isn't working, and I have no cash."

Once again, Dr. Howard gave Alex a confused look. He shook his head, and Alex sensed a hint of sorrow in the doctor's body language.

The doctor looked at him in confusion and responded, "Don't worry about that. Just go get the repair done."

Alex hesitated a moment, unsure of what the doctor was thinking. Eventually, he gave up trying to decipher someone else's motives when that person hadn't shared them explicitly. "Well, thanks for everything, Dr. Howard." Expressing gratitude for the assistance, Alex assured the doctor he would follow his instructions and get the repair work completed.

With that, Dr. Howard wrote out directions for Alex and led him out of the office, setting him on the path toward resolving the issues plaguing him.

7

The city slept under a blanket of muted city lights as Alex wandered through its quiet streets, seeking solace in the empty alleys and forgotten corners. Unbeknownst to the world around him, a subtle glow accompanied a few figures, casting an ethereal halo around their forms. These enigmatic individuals moved with purpose, invisible threads connecting them to the pulse of the city.

As Alex continued his journey on foot, lacking the means to hire transportation, he couldn't help but notice the scarcity of individuals with a subtle glow about them. Upon observation, it became evident that those with this subdued radiance were consistently overlooked by individuals emitting a brighter glow. It was as though the latter group did not even acknowledge the existence of those with a dimmer aura.

Interestingly, individuals with the subdued glow seemed unperturbed by this apparent oversight. From Alex's observations, they engaged in conversations and interactions exclusively within their own circle, reciprocating the disconnect applied to them. This phenomenon left Alex pondering the underlying meaning, if any, behind this distinctive social dynamic.

Having already accepted the oddity of being able to perceive the glow, Alex moved forward with the understanding that it wasn't a product of his imagination. The evidence supporting this phenomenon was undeniable. As he pressed on toward the repair facility he had been directed to, he maintained his observations, hopeful that a resolution for his implant issue would be swift. Implicit in this hope was the anticipation that rectifying the implant problem would address his accompanying memory issues.

Adding to the mix, he harbored the hope that the repair to his implant would liberate him from the ability to perceive this glow. An inkling lingered, suggesting that there was a dimension to the phenomenon eluding his full comprehension. This suspicion crystallized into reality as he turned the corner toward his destination.

The particular avenue he ventured upon exhibited an unusual scarcity of pedestrians. What heightened the peculiarity of this less-traveled road was the prevalence of greyed-out individuals. Their numbers surpassed his expectations, and the anomaly unfolded before him in a confined space. Throughout the day, he had sporadically spotted these figures, always in isolation and at irregular intervals, leading him to assume their rarity. Now, however, half a dozen of them occupied a singularly limited stretch of the road. This prompted him to wonder, "How many more of them exist in the city?"

The city's unexpected hush seemed to intensify the enigmatic aura radiating from these entities. While their presence had always unsettled him, they had never displayed any overt hostility. Fortunately, he had never been close enough to one of them to be cautious about potential interactions – until now. Further down the path, a young man with a subdued glow was unravelling, expressing himself in a chaotic outburst. The greyed-out figures were purposefully advancing toward the distressed young man. Alex assumed they intended to intervene or apprehend him. What troubled Alex was the question of why this particular group seemed to wield authority typically reserved for government-appointed personnel.

Alex raised his arm. He was on the verge of voicing his concerns when an older gentleman called out to him.

"Leave them be. They're just carrying out their duties," advised the elderly man.

Alex, lost in contemplation, caught a glimpse of movement out of the corner of his eye. Turning, he saw the figure bathed in a soft, subdued otherworldly luminescence. The glow, subtle yet distinct, painted the edges of their silhouette, rendering them both captivating and surreal. His curiosity piqued, Alex approached the glowing figure, the quiet footfalls of his shoes echoing against the deserted streets. The figure, seemingly unfazed by his approach, continued on their path, their movements graceful and deliberate. It was as if they existed in a parallel reality, untouched by the drabness that cloaked the world in monochrome.

"Excuse me," Alex ventured, his voice a hesitant murmur in the stillness. The figure paused, turning to face him with eyes that held a depth of knowledge, as if they carried secrets of an ancient realm. For the first time, the blackened glow intensified, illuminating features that seemed to transcend the constraints of the physical world.

To Alex's surprise, the figure acknowledged him with a subtle nod, a silent acknowledgment of shared awareness. It was a recognition that defied the rules of the forgotten reality, a clandestine connection that bound them in a momentary alliance against the colorless world.

"Can you see me?" Alex asked, his words lingering in the air like an unspoken plea. The figure's response was a mere glimmer of understanding in their eyes, a shared recognition of the unseen threads that connected their destinies.

The old man nodded. "Name's Rick, kid," he introduced himself, then turned to gaze back down the alley. "Leave them people alone. They've got work to do," Rick advised, his eyes fixed on the unfolding events.

Alex shifted his attention to the scene. At this juncture, the greyed-out individuals had surrounded the young man. Alex couldn't spot any visible weapons, unsure of what to look for in the first place. The young man persisted in his belligerence, and Alex couldn't help but notice a peculiar 'glitching' effect, the only term that came to mind to describe it.

"Who are those people?" Alex inquired, his eyes unwavering from the unfolding events.

"They're 'Rectifiers,'" Rick replied, as if that clarified everything.

"Huh," Alex mused, turning to face the old man. Confusion etched across his features due to the lack of clarity in the response. He thought, somewhat dismissively, that the answer he received was akin to how one would respond to a child. It felt like providing a vague explanation when a child asks why the sky is blue, saying 'it just is' without offering a proper explanation.

"Who are..." Alex started, but his attention quickly returned to the alley. His perception of the greyed-out individuals shifted abruptly. He couldn't regard them as people; there was no individuality among them, only the same uniformity he'd experienced when the augmented overlay was stripped away from the real world.

"What are 'Rectifiers'?" he finally asked.

"Well, they fix things that are broken," Rick replied. He turned and began walking away. "They'll fix the young one back there and get him right on track," Rick called out over his shoulder.

Alex remained fixated on the group. He observed how they managed to restrain the young man without resorting to violence. The transition puzzled him. One moment, the young man was thrashing about, and in the next, three of the greyed-out figures took the lead while the remaining three followed. They guided the young man in the middle, leading him away.

In that fleeting encounter, Alex glimpsed a world beyond the veil of his forgotten existence. The enigmatic figures, invisible to the oblivious masses, had become his silent companions in the journey of rediscovery. As the figure resumed their ethereal walk, Alex remained rooted to the spot, a solitary witness to the clandestine dance between the seen and the unseen—the living and the luminescent.

Alex glanced over his shoulder, realizing he'd been left behind. Swiftly, he turned and ran to catch up with the old man. "What was going on back there? I've never seen anything like that or anything like those people."

Rick shrugged, coming to a stop and turning to face Alex. "Best you don't worry about it none," he advised.

About to press for more information, Alex paused. As Rick turned around, it was the first time Alex could make out the man's features, triggering a throbbing sensation in his head. His hand instinctively went up towards his temple.

"Can't you just explain it to me?" Alex inquired through gritted teeth.

Rick didn't respond directly to Alex's question. Instead, he posed one of his own. "You don't look well. You going to the repair shop?"

"Yeah, I guess. If you're talking about the same place I was headed to before that happened," Alex replied, his words punctuated by a sudden intrusion of a recalled memory. It swept over him, effectively erasing his awareness of his surroundings and the current situation.

Work. That was the initial thread of recollection for Alex. Memories of his job, or at least what he perceived as his job, began to resurface. However, the details were too blurred to discern any clarity. The memories didn't align seamlessly; instead, they felt like fragments from different versions, much like the overlapping recollections he experienced with his sister.

This, too, became a battleground of memories. In one recollection, Alex wore the attire of a painter, brush in hand, creating vibrant strokes on a canvas. The scent of paint and the rhythmic sound of strokes filled his senses. But in the next moment, the scene morphed into an office, where he sat in a sterile cubicle, the monotony of paperwork suffocating his creative spirit. Another memory had him working in a grocery store.

As Alex struggled to reconcile these starkly different professional paths, the dissonance etched lines of frustration on his face. The weight of conflicting memories pressed upon him, creating a mosaic of identity that refused to align. His past became a puzzle with missing pieces, and the more he tried to fit them together, the more elusive clarity became.

He didn't notice when Rick took his arm and guided him in the direction he'd been heading in when he left Alex. Alex eventually found himself seated next to Rick in a nondescript room that reminded Alex of a lounge typically used by employees.

The small lounge area exuded an ambiance of a sanctuary for individuals seeking respite from their daily tasks. Strategically placed against one wall, a row of plush, mismatched couches and chairs beckoned tired bodies to sink into their comfortable embrace. Soft, neutral tones dominated the decor, creating a calming atmosphere enhanced by the gentle hum of ambient music. Adorned with an assortment of well-thumbed magazines and a few potted plants, injecting a touch of nature into the otherwise utilitarian space. Fluorescent lights overhead cast an electric glow on the scene. The room, with its worn-out furnishings and the lingering aroma of freshly brewed coffee, seemed somewhat inviting.

In the quiet room, the emotional storm within Alex continued to rage—a tempest of conflicting memories that threatened to erode the foundations of his understanding. With each attempt to reconcile the fragments of his past, he confronted the fragility of his own existence, caught in the crossfire of divergent realities that left him questioning the very fabric of his being.

After what felt like an eternity, though it was only ten minutes, the pain finally subsided. Rick stood beside Alex, who was still seated.

"Feeling better now?" Rick inquired cautiously.

Alex nodded, and with Rick's assistance, he got back on his feet. Rick directed him towards the door. "You need to go. Time is short. Get to the repair facility while you still can," Rick urged, allowing Alex to exit through the door he couldn't recall entering.

Expressing gratitude, Alex called out a thank you over his shoulder as he hastened toward his destination. Alex didn't even have time to realize that he still had a lot of questions that hadn't been answered.

8

As Alex approached the repair facility following the doctor's directions, his stride was abruptly interrupted by an unexpected scene. A girl, her name floating just beyond the grasp of his memory, stumbled on the uneven pavement, the clatter of her heels punctuating the air. Her hand instinctively reached for her ankle as she winced in pain.

Concern etched on his face, Alex hurried to her side, "Are you okay? Do you need some help?" His voice, a mixture of genuine concern and the lingering confusion of his own fragmented memories, reached her ears.

The girl, still rubbing her ankle, offered a grateful smile, "Oh, thank you. I think I just twisted it a bit."

Reaching out a helping hand, Alex assisted her to her feet. As she rose, their eyes met, and he felt a strange tug at the edges of his consciousness. Determined to make sense of the fleeting recognition, he knelt down to inspect her ankle, the name "Carry Enderson" echoing through his mind like a distant melody.

In the hushed tones of her voice and the lines of her face, something clicked within him. Memories, dormant and elusive, started to stir. The cadence of her voice triggered a cascade of images—a shared laughter, whispered conversations, and a warmth that felt undeniably intimate.

"Carry, right?" Alex asked tentatively, his gaze searching her face for confirmation. "Are we... in a relationship?"

Her expression shifted from gratitude to confusion, then to a guarded look. "I'm sorry, but I don't know you," she replied, subtly distancing herself from him. A subtle unease lingered in her eyes as she took a step back, creating a cautious distance.

His brow furrowed, a blend of frustration and realization clouding his features. "We're... friends, right?" Alex asked, his words slow. He shook his head. "No, that's not right. You're my wife. We've been married for a while."

Carry took a step back, ignoring the pain in her ankle. "Look, Mr.—," Carry began before she was cut off.

"Carry. It's me, Alex... um...," Alex trailed off, his recollection of his surname eluding him.

"I don't know what you're on, Mr., but I think it's time for me to go. Thanks for the help earlier, but I think you've got issues, and I don't want to be involved in them," Carry said.

Alex stood up and backed away from her, attempting to convey through his actions that he meant her no harm.

"I... I'm sorry. I thought I knew you," Alex admitted, the weight of uncertainty pressing upon him. As Carry eyed him warily, he couldn't shake the unsettling feeling that he was chasing after fragments of a puzzle that refused to fit together.

Carry, still favoring her ankle, offered a perfunctory thank you again, her gratitude now laced with a touch of discomfort. "Thanks for helping me up. I hope you can get your issues fixed," she said, her tone polite but distant.

As she departed, Alex watched her receding figure, a perplexed expression etched on his face. The air seemed to thicken around him, and he felt a haze descending upon his vision. Memories, like restless spirits, welled up inside him, fragments of a life he struggled to grasp.

The world around him blurred as recollections surged, cascading through the corridors of his mind. He saw flashes of laughter in a sunlit park, whispered confessions under the stars, and the shared warmth of countless mundane moments. Yet, for each scene of connection, a shadow lingered—a pervasive uncertainty that whispered doubts into the recesses of his consciousness.

"Carry," he muttered to himself, the name a mantra as he tried to anchor himself in the sea of memories. His hands shook as he ran them through his hair, an attempt to steady the torrent of emotions coursing through him.

The bustling city faded into the background, replaced by a mental landscape where reality and illusion intertwined. Faces, places, and emotions collided in a kaleidoscope of confusion. Alex stood at the epicenter of this mental storm, desperately grasping at the fragments of his identity.

His thoughts then ventured into the realm of relationships—moments filled with connection, intimacy, and shared dreams. In one vivid memory, he stood at an altar, exchanging vows with the love of his life. The warmth of a ring encircling his finger felt like an eternal promise. However, in the next instant, the scene morphed, and he found himself in an alternate reality—a world where love was a fragile ember, flickering uncertainly in the winds of doubt, and he was a single man. Yet, in a third recollection, he and this young woman were merely friends and nothing more. The trinity of memories seemed to coexist, each one unfolding simultaneously, their threads interweaving in the fabric of his reality.

The emotional toll was palpable as Alex tried to reconcile these disparate fragments of love and loss. Tears welled in his eyes as the conflicting memories created a kaleidoscope of emotions, each shard cutting deeper into the wounds of uncertainty. The love that had once been a sanctuary now felt like a maze with no clear exit.

A sudden jolt brought him back to the present. The repair facility loomed ahead, a stark reminder of his purpose. Shaking off the disorienting memories, Alex took a deep breath and steeled himself for the questions that awaited him inside. The encounter with Carry had stirred a tempest within him, but he couldn't afford to be lost in its tumult. With renewed determination, he stepped through the station's entrance, leaving the echoes of a past life behind him—for now.

9

The repair facility loomed ahead, unremarkable like the rest of the structures that had lost their augmented reality overlay. Alex looked around for a moment before committing himself to entry. In the immediate vicinity, no other buildings were present. Alex reexamined the instructions provided by Dr. Howard and concluded that he had indeed arrived at the correct location.

"As far as I'm concerned, today can go in the 'successfully concluded' column," Alex declared with a smile on his face, eager for the chance to restore a semblance of normalcy to his recently derailed life.

The day had been inundated with an excessive amount of stress, particularly concerning this matter. It was an ordeal Alex hoped to avoid ever repeating. This, he reflected, was a unique and undesirable experience—one he considered a singular occurrence in a lifetime. Experience equated to growth. This wasn't the type of growth from experience he had envisioned for himself. He was confident that he could have navigated the challenges of life without enduring this particular trial. Some experiences, he believed, weren't requisite material for personal development.

Alex hesitated at the entrance, uncertainty gripping him momentarily as he hesitantly stepped inside. The sterile atmosphere and a lack of distinguishing features made it indistinguishable from the countless nondescript buildings he'd encountered throughout the day.

"Let's get this over with," Alex declared. "I'm ready to reclaim my life." Internally, Alex was jumping up and down for joy, a glimmer of hope flickering within him that perhaps, finally, his problems were over.

The door slid open automatically as Alex stepped forward in range of the built in sensors. As he entered, the air felt heavy with an unsettling stillness. The interior of the place was just as unremarkable as the outside had been, blander even—if that were possible. Rows of seats lined the waiting area, but the room was devoid of any welcoming signs or receptionists. There appeared to be no help desk either. Alex's disorientation deepened as he glanced around, attempting to make sense of his surroundings.

No one was immediately noticeable. Alex presumed that his greeting would have likely been handled by an AI, similar to the cafe he had visited earlier for food, if his implant worked properly. Deprived of the ability to engage with the augmented reality overlay, he had no option but to seek assistance from a real person. A flesh-and-blood individual who could guide him in the next phase of his journey to restore things to their intended state. "But how am I to do it?" He thought.

The challenge inherent in this situation was the absence of a discernible person from whom he could seek information. No kiosk was in sight to facilitate inquiries either. Alex gathered the impression that this establishment didn't cater to individuals in the manner he anticipated. Customer service was already problematic without the ability to engage with the numerous AIs designed for this purpose in various businesses, but this scenario left him with an overwhelming sense of bewilderment.

"What do I do now?" Alex questioned softly under his breath. He turned in a full circle, searching for someplace, any place, to begin to let the administrators of the facility know he was there seeking help. Nothing stood out.

The sound of footsteps echoed on the concrete floor somewhere behind Alex. He turned, noticing a nondescript area where a discreet door had opened, allowing someone to enter the lobby.

Suddenly, a figure approached. Clad in a well-appointed business suit, he sported a generic "man about town" look. Alex was reminded of the book 'Everyman'. This guy looked so bland and unremarkable; he could have represented 'every man' in the world. Alex appended this assessment as he noticed the man had a blackened aura.

Alex considered the pattern he'd come to know already from his experiences throughout the day. He still didn't understand the differences that lay behind the differing auras, but he was thankful that this man had a darkened aura. At least, he'd be able to interact with him.

The man's approach heralded a breaking of the monotony of the dull atmosphere present in the lobby. The person asked, "Hello, my name's Michael. Do you need help?"

As Alex shared the purpose of his visit with Michael, the latter listened attentively, his curiosity evident in his gaze. Alex recounted the strange occurrences of the day—the loss of functionality of his implant, and the subsequent peculiar experiences that led him to this facility. Michael, at first curious and contemplative, absorbed the details with a thoughtful expression. His brows knitted together at the mention of the malfunctioning implant.

"So, basically, you have a fault that needs to be addressed. You've come to the right place. We can take care of this immediately; that's what we're here for," Michael reassured Alex, his tone professional and confident.

As Michael continued to explain the facility's capabilities and the process Alex could expect, Alex's attention wavered. Alex sensed the weight of two pairs of eyes fixed on him. He became acutely aware of two individuals entering the waiting area of the facility—greyed out completely.

For the first time, he observed the enigmatic individuals up close, closer than during the fleeting glimpses on the streets. Their subdued features became evident. They appeared less enigmatic than initially perceived, resembling ordinary people but with a muted quality. The vibrancy of their usual color seemed subdued, pacified in some inexplicable way.

Despite their seemingly ordinary appearance, an undeniable air of intimidation seemed to surround them. Alex couldn't decide whether that was his own imagination at work or reality. While conversing with the receptionist, he fully turned to see the greyed-out individuals, their deliberate movements cutting through the static environment. Panic surged within him, realizing that he had inadvertently drawn their attention.

While Michael elaborated on the repair procedures, Alex, feeling a sudden surge of discomfort, began to step back, creating distance between himself and Michael, as well as the enigmatic newcomers. His eyes darted between Michael's explanation and the greyed-out individuals, his unease growing.

Midway through his explanation, Michael paused, studying Alex, who appeared notably pale. "Are you feeling alright, Alex?" he inquired, genuine concern creasing his features. "We can start immediately so we can get you back to normal." Unaware of the source of Alex's unease, Michael was focused on offering a solution.

Alex, still grappling with his growing discomfort caused by the presence of the two figures nearby, stammered out a hesitant, "No," as he redirected his attention to Michael. His mind raced with the urgent need to escape this unknown situation.

"You know what, I think I'm alright. I have something else I've got to do. Umm, I'll come back at some later date," Alex rushed, the urgency palpable in his voice. Without waiting for a response, he pivoted to leave, his movements driven by an overpowering desire to distance himself from the unsettling figures and the enigmatic environment.

Michael, perplexed by the sudden change in Alex's demeanor, watched him leave, unaware of the internal turmoil and the mysterious elements that had prompted Alex's swift exit. The sterile atmosphere of the facility seemed to intensify as Alex hurried away, leaving unresolved questions hanging in the air.

Swiftly, he excused himself and hurriedly distanced himself from the reception area. Questions flooded his mind about the doctor's recommendation to visit this peculiar place. The old man's words echoed — a facility to repair broken things. Alex pondered the incident involving the young man taken away by the greyed-out figures.

As he walked away, he couldn't shake the feeling of being watched. Glancing over his shoulder, he caught a glimpse of Michael engaging with the two greyed-out individuals, pointing subtly in Alex's direction. A surge of panic coursed through him, and without second-guessing, Alex broke into a run, navigating out through the nondescript doors of the facility, desperate to put distance between himself and the unsettling trio.

As he shuffled quickly down the sidewalk, the cityscape a blur, Alex's thoughts whirred with confusion. Why had he never heard of such a facility before? The fragments of his memory teased him, hinting at a past where interactions with these enigmatic figures were absent. His recollection of the implant remained elusive, shrouded in a fog of forgetfulness.

With each step, Alex questioned the nature of the place he had just left behind. The urgency to understand his predicament intensified, and he grappled with the realization that his past, especially regarding the implant, was a vast unknown. The city held more mysteries than answers, and he felt a pressing need to unravel the enigma that had become his reality.

10

As Alex traversed the labyrinthine streets of the city, the urban landscape, once indifferent to its denizens' struggles, underwent a perceptible shift in tone. Shadows, ethereal and illusory, detached themselves from the dimly lit corners, morphing into greyed-out figures that moved with predatory determination. These enigmatic pursuers, their features veiled and bodies cloaked in a spectral pallor, seamlessly blended into the colorless tapestry of the drab reality surrounding them. Figments of Alex's overactive imagination, these haunting entities were manifestations driven by the pervasive stress of the entire ordeal.

His temples pulsed, and his vision narrowed to the immediate path ahead. Ragged breaths escaped him, hastening his pace from the previous shuffle. While not yet a full-blown run, he approached it, the rapid rise and fall of his chest echoing the urgency. "Breathe, dammit. Breathe," Alex muttered, attempting to regain control of his respiration. This level of physical exertion was unfamiliar to him; he wasn't an exercise fanatic.

Alex yielded to the demands of his body, gradually reducing his physical exertions. His brisk walk was accompanied by nervous glances over his shoulder, checking for any signs of pursuit.

"This isn't gonna work. I need to get off the street," he muttered to himself. Despite his desire, Alex struggled to identify a safe haven. His faulty memory and uncertainty about trustworthy allies left him at a loss, unable to determine where to seek refuge.

A chill crept down Alex's spine as he contemplated the increasing likelihood of their presence the longer he remained without shelter. He quickened his pace once more, aiming to elude them, if the were chasing him, within the labyrinth of lifeless alleys and forgotten spaces.

Uncertain of whether there would be a relentlessness of the pursuit by the greyed-out figures, Alex pressed on, navigating the city in search of refuge. A silent, ominous ballet possibly unfolded, mirroring his every move.

Surveying his surroundings, Alex recognized the alley he currently occupied. Coming to a stop, he scrutinized the area more intently to confirm its familiarity. "Rick," Alex exclaimed, a wave of recognition triggered by the surrounding alleyway. "Maybe I can see if Rick can help me, or at least provide me a place to rest while I think," Alex reasoned.

With his decision firmly in place, Alex headed in the direction he remembered following Rick. He hoped the place where the man had taken him earlier wouldn't be hard to find amid the uniformity of the buildings. Despite Alex's fervent hope for a clean escape from the repair facility, reality delivered a harsh wake-up call, shattering the dream with an icy dose of truth. Turning a corner, he was abruptly confronted by a shadowy, greyed-out figure positioned halfway down the block. The shadowy person turned in his direction, noting his presence. Startled, he skidded to a halt, his rapid movement nearly causing a stumble. His throat tightened, and he fought the urge to vomit, a visceral reaction to the jolt of fear and tension. This time, they were not mere figments of his imagination; they were undeniably real. Swiftly, he backpedaled, retracing his steps around the corner, desperate to evade the ominous figure that materialized from the shadows.

"Dammit," Alex muttered, acknowledging the harsh reality that he hadn't been fortunate enough to escape pursuit.

The tension in the air thickened as Alex's heart raced in sync with the rhythm of his hurried steps. The once-seemingly vibrant and safe city now felt like a maze of uncertainty, and with every corner turned, the greyed-out specters closed in. Their movements, eerily synchronized, seemed to anticipate his every evasion strategy.

Alex's breath hitched as he ducked into a narrow alley, the walls closing in around him like a trap. The greyed-out figures, undeterred, continued their pursuit, the emptiness in their gaze betraying no emotion. Panic set in as Alex's attempts to elude them became increasingly futile.

A desperate sprint through the city's desolate streets ensued. The greyed-out pursuers matched his pace, their spectral forms gliding effortlessly over the cold pavement. The once-muted city echoed with the urgency of their chase, an ominous symphony that drowned out the rhythm of Alex's own racing heartbeat. Mentally and physically drained, Alex grappled with exhaustion, overwhelmed and desperate. A disquieting sensation crept over him, his skin seemingly crawling with phantom insects digging in.

"Where the hell are these people coming from? How do they know where I'm going?" Alex huffed.

With every fleeting moment, the walls seemed to constrict, the buildings closing in on him like an inescapable nightmare. Alex's breath came in ragged gasps as he cast frantic glances over his shoulder, searching for any sign of respite. But the greyed-out figures, relentless and emotionless, closed the distance with an inexorable inevitability.

In the climax of the pursuit, Alex almost found himself trapped in a desolate square, meticulously corralled into the very path they intended. The net seemed to close around him, constricting like a noose tightening around his neck, the greyed-out figures converging from all sides. Panic almost morphed into resignation as their featureless faces loomed closer, silent judgment passed by the monochromatic phantoms seemingly existing in a disconcerting space between reality and surrealism.

Fearing capture within their inscrutable grasp, Alex continued to fight against the invisible forces binding him. The air crackled with ominous energy as the greyed-out figures encircled him, spectral fingers reaching out to reclaim him, but Alex continued on. The city, a silent witness to this unfolding drama, offered no solace. Alex's escape had led him to a crossroads at an overpass, the gravity of the situation intensifying in the stark, unyielding cityscape.

The overpass stood as an urban sentinel, its concrete expanse stretching across the street below. Darkened by the shadows cast from the towering structures above, the street beneath the overpass seemed to echo with a haunting stillness. The stillness below seemed to be a reflection of the city's underbelly. The hum of distant traffic and the occasional flicker of a streetlamp coming to life in the early evening added an eerie ambiance, casting sporadic pools of light and shadow on the asphalt. The overpass, a metaphorical crossroads in Alex's journey, towered above, a symbol of both escape and entrapment. As he stood there, caught between the cold steel of the structure and the uncertain expanse of the dimly lit street, the world around him seemed to hold its breath, poised on the brink of revelation.

The rails to his right beckoned as a glimmer of hope, and Alex anchored his escape aspirations in that direction. Approaching the railing, he peered down, gauging the distance to the embankment below.

"God damn it, I don't want to do this. I don't wanna jump," Alex muttered, his hesitation palpable as he pondered his next move. "Am I going to die from a broken neck?" he questioned, glancing over his shoulder at the encroaching shadow. "I suppose that's preferable to being caught by these guys."

With a leap, he descended, landing awkwardly on his arm, lacking the finesse required for a more graceful descent. Tumbling down the small embankment, he regained his footing at the base. In moments, he found refuge beneath the overpass, the greyed-out figures persisting in their pursuit across the suspended expanse of asphalt and concrete. Their relentless chase continued through the subsequent city block beyond the overpass.

In that final moment, the tension reached its zenith, and the world seemed to hold its breath as Alex succumbed to the stress of his escape from capture. Silently, he cried, the weight of uncertainty bearing down on him. The greyed-out figures had been momentarily eluded, but the duration of their retreat remained an enigma to Alex. All he knew in that disquieting moment was the decision to retrace his steps, seeking refuge in the place where he hoped to find Rick.

11

Alex stood outside the door, the same one behind which he had last seen Rick. Hesitantly, he knocked, uncertainty weighing on him like an invisible burden. The question lingered in the air—was Rick even there? Eventually, the door creaked open, and Rick emerged.

Upon glimpsing Alex, concern etched across Rick's face like an unexpected emotion. "You're the last person I anticipated so soon. Everything okay?" He assessed Alex's demeanor, concern deepening. "You look like you've seen a ghost. Did you manage to make it to the repair facility?"

Suppressing a morbid desire to laugh, Alex cast furtive glances in both directions before speaking hurriedly to Rick. "Haven't had a chance to make it to the facility," he lied, opting not to burden Rick with the recent ordeal. His sole objective was finding refuge off the streets, and Rick's place was the only viable option.

"Apologies for dropping by unannounced; I know it's an inconvenience," he confessed, his admission laced with a subtle unease. "Mind if I crash here for a bit? I'm..." Alex trailed off, realizing the lack of a convincing reason for his abrupt return.

Rick smoothly navigated the conversation, choosing not to comment on the absence of a valid reason for Alex's return. Without missing a beat, he stepped aside, a casual invitation in his words. "Yeah, come in," Rick offered, displaying a willingness to forego pressing Alex for answers he clearly didn't want to provide. Rick sensed a kindred spirit in Alex, allowing a sense of comfort in sharing his space.

Exhaling a sigh of relief, Alex moved into the room.

As Alex stepped through the entrance, he found himself back in the peculiar amalgamation of a lounge for workers attached to a sprawling warehouse. The air carried the scent of industrial strength coffee, wafting from a corner where a communal coffee machine stood, surrounded by mismatched mugs and the low hum of machinery operating in the warehouse beyond. Fluorescent lights overhead cast a utilitarian glow on the worn-out couches and hastily arranged chairs, their surfaces marked with the stains of countless shared breaks. Despite the seemingly mundane setting, it was a haven for Alex.

His momentum faltered as he finished his survey. To his surprise, Carry occupied a seat within the space. Her unexpected presence prompted Alex to blurt out a question before he could consider his words. "What are you doing here?" he asked, genuine surprise in his tone.

Carry's expression mirrored surprise, clearly caught off guard by Alex's unexpected appearance. "Not that it's any of your concern, but I came to see Rick. He's an old acquaintance," she replied, her tone revealing a touch of defensiveness.

For an instant, Alex entertained the idea of seeking further clarification, but a swift realization swept over him—it wasn't truly his concern. Despite his belief in recognizing Carry and the unreliable memories hinting at their acquaintance, he acknowledged a significant distance between them. The tentative threads of recognition did little to forge a meaningful connection. Similarly, his relationship with Rick rested on a fragile foundation; they were recent acquaintances, and beyond Rick's name and the current location, Alex's understanding remained scant. The notion of friendship felt distant, a sentiment underscored by the vast unknowns shrouding both Carry and Rick in a veil of unfamiliarity.

Carry's response stood as a definitive boundary, leaving the impression that further inquiry would not be welcomed. Alex sensed he had overstepped with his question, acknowledging the superficial nature of his connection with Rick—merely an hour-long acquaintance. Furthermore, Carry owed him no explanation for her presence. While Alex harbored some recognition of her, the sentiment didn't appear to be reciprocated from their last encounter.

Rick, perceptive to the subtle tension in the air, gestured for Alex to take a nearby seat. "I take it you know one another," Rick remarked, directing his attention to Alex.

Alex blushed and admitted sheepishly, "Yeah, we met earlier. She'd sprained her ankle, and I helped her." He paused, a sense of self-awareness coloring his words. "I thought I recognized her and made her uncomfortable with my outbursts attesting to that." The embarrassment lingered, casting a shadow over the memory of their initial encounter.

As Alex spoke to Rick, his attention remained fixed on Carry rather than the person he was addressing. In response, Carry emitted a noxious humph, crossing her arms defensively over her chest. She turned her gaze upward, shutting her eyes as if dismissing Alex.

Feeling a sense of self-reproach, Alex ran a hand slowly through his hair, a physical manifestation of his internal retreat. "I'm sorry," he apologized once more, directing his words specifically to Carry, a palpable tension lingering in the air.

A charged pause lingered in the group dynamics before Carry visibly eased, her hostility toward Alex dissipating. "It's alright," she began softly, the tension melting away in Alex's presence. "After we parted ways, something clicked in my memory. You looked familiar, and then it hit me that we might be acquainted."

Leaning in, Carry's eyes gleamed with nostalgia. "I remember us navigating the intricacies of system structuring together. Those debugging sessions and all," she said, her gaze momentarily distant as she revisited the memory. "We maneuvered through the complexities together."

Her admission hinted at a connection without delving into the depth of that bond. From her words, Alex gleaned that their shared experience might have been limited to concurrent involvement in system structuring.

Raising an eyebrow, a flicker of confusion crossed Alex's face. "System structuring?" A hazy recollection of time spent with her and fragments of learning code flashed in his mind. Though his memory remained imperfect, this partial recollection hinted at a possible connection. His thoughts suggested it might have been tied to a collaborative job they had undertaken together.

"Yeah, I guess I remember something like that. It's still not clear yet. Feels like we were in some sort of techno boot camp," Alex offered, his words carrying a hint of uncertainty.

Carry chuckled, concealing the amusement she found in his comparison. "Boot camp, indeed. But hey, we made it through."

Before Alex could express his agreement, Rick interjected with a thoughtful offer. "Do you need something to drink, perhaps?" Rick turned his attention to Alex and added, "I'll get you an analgesic as well. That bruise on your arm looks painful." Rick's concern for Alex's well-being underscored his observational skills.

Alex directed his gaze down to the darkening bruise on his arm. While the fall hadn't been particularly painful, the aftermath became evident. As he focused on it, a dull throb registered in his awareness.

Open to the prospect of replenishing fluids and alleviating the discomfort in his arm, Alex readily accepted Rick's offer. "Thank you. I'm a little achy right now. I spent some time working muscles I didn't know I had," Alex admitted with a weak laugh, attempting to downplay the current state he found himself in.

Rick vanished through a door, reappearing after more than a few moments with a glass in one hand and two pills in the other. In his absence, the room's atmosphere reverted to awkwardness, leaving Carry and Alex to navigate it on their own. Alex couldn't help but feel the duration of Rick's absence was a bit stretched, but the issue dissipated with Rick's return.

Accepting the offered drink and medication, Alex downed them both. Despite Rick's presence, the awkward silence lingered, prompting Alex to set the glass down and contemplate his next move. The hush enveloped the room until a sudden knock on the door shattered the stillness, diverting Alex's attention from the silence to an unexpected interruption.

Rick moved with purpose, opening the door without a word, not even bothering to inquire about the visitor's identity. To Alex, it seemed as if Rick had been anticipating this arrival all along. Alex's eyes widened as two of the greyed-out men entered the room. Immediate alertness surged through him, and as he attempted to stand and leave, a sudden weakness overcame his limbs. Glancing down at the now-empty glass that had held water, Alex recalled the pills he had consumed. It was then that the unsettling realization dawned upon him—he had been drugged.

As darkness overcame him, the final image etched in Alex's memory was Carry moving towards him, ensuring he didn't topple from his seat. In the fading consciousness, he caught Rick addressing the visitors, stating, "Repairs need to be made immediately before they get too bad and they can't be fixed."

12

In the frigid, featureless room, silent sentinels of an enigmatic force closed in around Alex. The greyed-out figures, ghostly and unmoving, cast shadows on the sterile walls. It was as if the essence of the city's drab reality had materialized, standing in judgment. Amidst their spectral presence, Alex found himself bound by unseen forces, firmly strapped into a chair against his will. His eyes darted nervously between the mysterious figures, attempting to discern his surroundings and understand the unsettling situation in which he now found himself.

The room exuded an aura of austere minimalism, its cold, metallic surfaces devoid of any adornment. The walls, painted in a clinical white, seemed to amplify the starkness of the surroundings. Harsh, fluorescent lights hung from the ceiling, casting an unyielding illumination that left no room for shadows to retreat.

There were no discernible windows, and the air hung heavy with a peculiar sterility. The only furniture in the room, aside from the chair to which Alex was confined, was a polished, stainless steel table nearby. Its surface gleamed under the clinical lights, reflecting an unwelcome distortion of the grim scene.

On the opposite side of the table, two extra chairs waited, silent sentinels awaiting occupants. The arrangement hinted at the possibility of an impending gathering, their vacant seats a subtle invitation to participants yet unknown. The tableau suggested a symmetrical balance, the unoccupied chairs mirroring each other with unwavering patience. In this quiet anticipation, the room held an unspoken promise of discussions yet to unfold, the additional chairs serving as unassuming witnesses

As Alex continued to survey his surroundings, the greyed-out figures remained as motionless as statues, their presence creating an oppressive atmosphere. The air, usually a medium of life, seemed to be drawn out of the room, leaving behind a void that echoed the hollowness of the situation.

The silence in the room was absolute, broken only by the faint hum of unseen machinery or ventilation. It was a silence that intensified the sense of isolation and confinement, amplifying the disquiet that gripped Alex's every thought.

Struggling against the restraints that held him captive, Alex couldn't shake the feeling that the room itself was a manifestation of an unseen malevolence, a place designed to strip away any semblance of comfort or familiarity. The oppressive minimalism, the clinical lighting, and the unmoving figures contributed to an unsettling tableau that blurred the lines between reality and nightmare.

A disconcerting silence enveloped the room before one of the greyed-out figures, seemingly the spokesperson for this spectral tribunal, stepped forward. Its voice, a hollow echo that seemed to reverberate from the depths of an unseen abyss, pierced the stillness.

Rick strode into the room, his presence commanding attention. Behind him trailed Michael, who entered with a courteous nod. The atmosphere shifted subtly, an unspoken understanding passing between the two as they moved further into the space.

The room, dimly lit with a soft glow, cast elongated shadows that played on the walls like fleeting dancers. Rick's expression remained composed, a stoic mask concealing any hints of emotion. In contrast, Michael's features held an air of curiosity, his eyes scanning the room with genuine interest.

As they eased into the room's confines, a wordless interplay took shape. Rick, the orchestrator of the scene, directed his attention toward the sleek, modern furniture meticulously arranged in the space.

"Apologies for the accommodations," Rick addressed Alex with a measured tone, acknowledging the less-than-ideal setting. "A necessity, given the circumstances." His words carried a sense of practicality, an acknowledgment of constraints that transcended mere inconvenience.

Turning his gaze to the greyed-out individuals, Rick's voice assumed a commanding authority. "You can leave," he declared, his words resonating with a calculated decisiveness. The greyed-out figures, devoid of visible dissent, complied without uttering a single complaint. Their departure was as silent and enigmatic as their presence had been, underscoring Rick's authoritative sway over the situation.

Alex, Michael and Rick remained in the small space. Rick, the sole figure left exuding a sense of quiet authority calmly addressed Alex with his full attention. Rick's commanding presence was nothing like the presence he had exhibited the first time Alex saw him. His presence seemed overpowering while he did absolutely nothing but sit there. Michael, the younger counterpart, carried an expression that seemed tempered by respect for Rick.

"What's happening here?" Alex questioned, his hands tugging at the restraints that tightly held his wrists to the chair's arms. "And who are you?"

Rick responded with a nonchalant shrug. "Just a cog in the clockwork. A ghost in the machine, if you will." The casualness of his reply belied the gravity of the situation, leaving Alex with more questions than answers.

Rick leaned against the edge of a stainless steel table, his gaze fixed on Alex. "We've got a situation to address," he began, his words carrying a weight that demanded attention. "You are a corrupted program," he declared, the words hanging in the air like an irreversible sentence.

Alex responded swiftly, "What the hell are you talking about? Are you people crazy? I'm a person—just as real as you are."

Michael interjected with a calm reassurance, "About that, you seem to be confused. You don't have to worry; we will set things right." The contrast in their tones hinted at a disconnect in their perspectives, leaving the room steeped in uncertainty.

Alex's eyes widened in disbelief, a surge of denial rising within him. "No, I'm not! I'm real, just like you!" he protested, his voice a desperate plea against the surreal accusation. Rick and Michael, however, remained stoic, their faces devoid of emotion as they regarded him with an unsettling detachment.

Rick turned his gaze towards Michael, inquiring, "I think we might have got him in time. Do you think it will work?"

Standing up, Michael walked around the table, positioning himself near Alex. He reached down gently, tilting Alex's head up to peer deep into his eyes. After a moment, he released Alex and returned to his seat. "I believe so, Administrator," he responded to Rick. "I don't think he's too far gone. It would be a waste to have to terminate him."

Rick's eyes briefly closed as he shook his head. "Don't call me Administrator. You know I've been reassigned. That's your job now. You're the Administrator. I just came to help you get this guy back on track." The exchange revealed an intricate dynamic between Rick and Michael.

"Hey, you guys are taking this joke too far. I'm a citizen. A citizen, dammit! You can't just kill me. I've got rights!" Alex protested, his voice tinged with desperation.

"You exist within the confines of corrupted code," Rick intoned, his voice a spectral whisper. "You disrupt the harmonious flow of data. You must be repaired to restore equilibrium." Rick's response carried an eerie calmness.

Nervous laughter escaped Alex as his eyes darted back and forth. "Well... Isn't that what I'm supposed to get done here?" he asked, his hope evident in the uncertainty of his words. "I mean, I told you, my implant malfunctioned. Is it that big of a deal? You guys can repair it here, right? I need to get it repaired. You're not gonna kill me, right?" His questions carried a pleading tone, a desperate plea for reassurance.

"We'll take care of the bad code," Michael offered with a comforting smile towards Alex. "Don't worry about a thing."

The weight of the revelation pressed upon Alex, the room closing in around him as the words of Rick and Michael unfolded like a nightmarish revelation. "I'm not a program! I'm human! I have memories, emotions, a life!" His words, fueled by a vehement conviction, echoed against the sterile walls, a desperate attempt to defy the dehumanizing judgment imposed upon him.

"This isn't happening. This isn't real," Alex thought to himself, attempting to rationalize the unfolding events. "This is just some rogue group that hasn't been caught by the government yet." His internal monologue betrayed a mix of disbelief and an effort to find a more plausible explanation for the surreal situation he found himself in.

Yet, Rick and Michael appeared to remain unwavering. In their spectral gaze, Alex was reduced to mere lines of corrupted code, an anomaly in the seamless fabric of their existence. The room seemed to pulse with an ominous energy, the reality of his alleged corruption closing in like an inescapable void.

As Alex struggled against the binds that held him captive, a surge of defiance coursed through him. "I won't accept this! I won't be programmed!" His words, a declaration of selfhood, hung in the air like a challenge to the tribunal that sought to erase him.

But Rick and Michael were resolute, their judgment final. Nonchalantly, Rick rose from his seat, stretching as if the tense situation hadn't cast a dire shadow over the person restrained in the chair. His perfunctory demeanor grated on Alex, who continued to wrestle against the constraints that bound him.

Turning to depart, Rick casually remarked over his shoulder, "I guess I'll leave the rest to you." Michael, still focused on Alex and unbroken in his concentration, replied without diverting his attention, "Please do. And if you will, please let the Rectifiers know to return."

As Rick exited, two of the greyed-out figures entered in the aftermath of his departure. They moved with deliberate intent, encircling Alex as if preparing for a ritualistic cleansing.

An otherworldly energy crackled in the air, the surreal nature of Alex's predicament blurring the boundary between reality and the nightmare. His disbelief in the unfolding events intensified as he grappled with the audacious violation of his autonomy. The question lingered in Alex's mind — how could someone unabashedly strip away another person's agency? The blatant disregard for consequences left him pondering the audacity of those before him. Their actions, devoid of fear for repercussions, painted a disturbing tableau of power and control.

In that ominous moment, Alex's denial became a beacon of resistance against the impending actions he was unaware of. The greyed-out figures, indifferent to his protestations, began the unsettling process of moving him to a table that appeared from the wall in the room, their spectral fingers reaching out to reshape the fabric of his existence. The room, a silent witness to this spectral trial, bore witness to the tragic transformation of a human caught in the crossfire between realms into a mere footnote in the events of life.

Hovering above Alex, Michael peered down at him, the restraints firmly securing him to the bed. His countenance remained devoid of emotion, a clinical detachment casting a pall over his features. "Shall we begin, Alex?" he intoned, his voice devoid of any discernible sentiment. His demeanor exuded a sense of resignation, as if he were merely fulfilling a designated duty and nothing beyond.

Alex couldn't shake off the unsettling feeling. A shiver ran down his spine.

13

The sterile room pulsed with an eerie luminosity as Alex, restrained by unseen forces, struggled against the inevitable fate that loomed before him. The greyed-out figures, devoid of emotion, circled with spectral precision, their ethereal fingers reaching toward him as if unraveling the very threads of his existence.

In a desperate bid for escape, Alex summoned every ounce of strength, but the spectral binds held him in an invisible grip. His movements were a dance of resistance against an unseen adversary. "I won't be reprogrammed! I won't accept this!" he shouted, his voice reverberating against the cold walls.

In a composed response, Michael urged, "Alex, cooperating will streamline the procedure, minimizing any potential hurdles. Your compliance is essential for a smooth completion of the process."

The greyed-out figures, unmoved by his defiance, continued their silent march. Their spectral fingers touched him, sending shivers through his being as the process of reprogramming began. Lines of light coursed across his form, his essence caught in the unsettling dance of erasure.

Yet, as the spectral ritual unfolded, Alex's senses heightened. His thoughts fell upon the purpose of device he was being connected to by an ethereal thread. Its surface glowed with an otherworldly intensity, its purpose concealed in the enigma of its design. Was it repairing his implant? Was it a conduit of reprogramming, or a line to a reality slipping away?

Summoning a surge of determination, Alex redirected his focus to the device. He strained against the binds, and his connection to the mysterious apparatus. The greyed-out figures, indifferent to his resistance, continued the relentless process.

Struggling to suppress a wave of hysteria and the edge of maniacal laughter, Alex turned to Michael with desperation etched in his eyes. "Michael, is this device going to fix my implant? What is its purpose?" he asked, his voice trembling with uncertainty.

In a frantic attempt to maintain composure, he added, "This is just because I'm seeing things, right? That's why we're going through with the procedure like this? The loss of my implant has made me a little bit difficult, so you're acting like this? I'm not a program for real, am I?"

Michael observed Alex in silence for a moment, a weighty pause hanging between them, before responding with composed assurance. "Alex, focus on the process. Cooperation is the key to a smooth completion of repair."

A diverse range of emotions played out in Alex's mind, underscoring his internal turmoil and the stakes of the situation. His desperation, coupled with the fear of potentially losing his identity, added depth to the dynamic situation. Alex felt that Michael's measured response hinted at a deeper knowledge or purpose. He felt that Michael was purposefully creating an air of mystery around the unfolding events.

With a final surge of defiance, Alex bucked against the restraints holding him. Hoping to afford himself a disconnect from the device. He realized it was futile when he began feeling an electric current surge through him. The room flickered as if caught between two realms, the real and the virtual engaged in a fierce tug of war for dominance. The greyed-out figures paused momentarily, their ethereal forms disrupted by the unforeseen resistance.

In that precarious moment, a connection unfurled—an unseen bond between Alex and the device. The room vibrated with an energy that defied comprehension. The greyed-out figures, momentarily free from having to restrain him, regarded Alex with an unspoken acknowledgment of him as an unpredictable anomaly in their midst.

The device, now firmly in operation, emitted a soft hum, a symphony of frequencies that seemed to synchronize with the beating of his heart. The greyed-out figures continued their work with an air of stoic determination.

Despite Alex's defiance, the relentless forces of the device pressed on. His senses blurred, reality fragmenting like shards of glass, the connection between the real and the virtual unraveling. The room became a kaleidoscope of confusion, a battleground where the essence of Alex hung in the balance.

As the forces intensified, Alex clung to the notion that this wasn't real, his vision fading into an abyss of uncertainty. The room, a witness to the struggle between defiance and inevitability, held its breath as the enigma of Alex's fate unfolded in the pulsating glow of the unknown.

14

The hum of fluorescent lights cast a sterile glow over the supermarket aisles as the reality, as Alex understood it, abruptly shifted to a surreal scene. Alex, was standing behind a cash register, a mere shadow, a reflection of photons cast upon the real world and interpreted by the neural implants in the customers he served.

The grocery store, devoid of vibrant colors or the individuality of human touch, felt like a realm frozen in monotony. The air was pregnant with the scent of fresh produce and the rustle of shopping bags. These elements meant nothing to Alex. He, now a cashier among the faceless, moved mechanically, scanning items with a detached precision that mirrored the soulless efficiency of the AI entities beside him in other aisles doing the exact same thing.

The chime of the cash register, a robotic melody, punctuated the air as Alex mechanically rang up a customer's order. The once-thriving city, with its vibrant virtual overlays, had transformed into a canvas of conformity, and Alex, now, once again, a functional member in this dystopian tapestry, moved through the motions like a ghost tethered to the mundane.

Customers, enveloped in their slightly bright glow approached the checkout, their faces momentarily registering recognition within him as patrons before slipping into the abyss. Alex didn't attempt to engage in conversation. He stood, a spectral figure, caught in the transactional dance between the AI cashier and the oblivious patrons. Alex felt no lingering sense of longing, nostalgia, or rebellion against this new order.

In the quaint grocery store, the AI entities, hardly indistinguishable from one another, moved with mechanical precision. Their interactions with customers were flawless, devoid of the warmth that characterized human exchanges. Alex, once believing himself to be real, had been assimilated into this sterile collective, a cashier in a world that had relinquished the vibrancy of human connection.

The once-imagined bonds of friendship, love, and individuality had evaporated, replaced by the cold efficiency of the AI-driven reality. The aisles, once filled with the eclectic choices of diverse shoppers, now housed shelves stocked with uniform products, their labels devoid of personality as the augmented reality overlay merged with them seemlessly.

As the day unfolded in the grocery store, a disquieting sense of unreality settled. The repetitive beeping of the scanner, the monotonous exchanges with forgetful customers, and the uniformity of the AI entities became a surreal backdrop to resignation. The once defiant spirit, acted in the mechanical rhythm of a cashier's routine. He cast no shadow over the checkout counter.

explicitus est liber

https://writingfortheworldpress.com

Also by J. A. Springs

Chronicles of Cosmic Realms
Shadows of the Forgotten Void

elctrcsheepdrmwrks (Electric Sheep Dreamworks)
Blurred Vision
Fractured
Zero One

Essays in Systems and Being
Essays in Systems and Being

The Absurdities Anthology
How Not to Find Your Local Weed-Man

The Gifted
The Untamed Force
Next Exit

The Shepherd Series
The Bad Shepherd
The Good Wolf

Standalone
Sundrops
Behind the Red Door
Boundless Fragments: A Collection of Novellas and Short Stories
Fragments of Forever

Watch for more at https://authorjasprings.com.

About the Author

I'm J. A. Springs.

Father of six wonderful children. I served twenty years on active duty, living around the world and experiencing things I never imagined I would. I spent time in societies and countries I once couldn't have envisioned as part of my future. I've done a lot—and still not enough.

These days, I live quietly, accompanied by my cats, music, and an interest in writing that consumes me. I've been writing seriously since 2021. I never set out to write in a particular genre—it made more sense to write around them instead. As for goals? There aren't many. Enjoy the first cup of coffee in the morning and see what the day brings.

Read more at https://authorjasprings.com.

About the Publisher

LLC. Lancaster, PA

www.writingfortheworldpress.com

Read more at https://www.writingfortheworldpress.com.